# JAN KARON

PRESENTS

❖ CYNTHIA COPPERSMITH'S ❖

## Violet Comes to Stay

story *by* MELANIE CECKA

pictures *by* EMILY ARNOLD McCULLY

VIKING

*For Regina Hayes and Joy Peskin, who believed with me*
*that this book by a fictitious creator could become real—J.K.*

*To Muriel Faxon at The Chatham Bookstore*
*and to Jean and Rondi at Blackwood and Brouwer—E.A.M.*

VIKING, Published by Penguin Group, Penguin Young Readers Group, 345 Hudson Street, New York, New York 10014, U.S.A. Penguin Books Ltd, Registered Offices: 80 Strand, London WC2R 0RL, England. First published in 2006 by Viking, a division of Penguin Young Readers Group. Text copyright © Jan Karon, 2006. Illustrations copyright © Emily Arnold McCully, 2006. All rights reserved. LIBRARY OF CONGRESS CATALOGING-IN-PUBLICATION DATA: Cecka, Melanie. Jan Karon presents Cynthia Coppersmith's Violet comes to stay: a Mitford storybook / story by Melanie Cecka ; pictures by Emily Arnold McCully.—1st ed. p. cm. Summary: Violet, a little white cat, tries out several homes before she finds just the right one. ISBN 0-670-06073-9 (hardcover) 〚1. Cats—Fiction. 2. Animals—Infancy—Fiction. 3. Dwellings—Fiction.〛 I. Karon, Jan, date- II. McCully, Emily Arnold, ill. III. Title. IV. Title: Cynthia Coppersmith's Violet comes to stay. V. Title: Violet comes to stay. PZ7.C29993Ja 2006 〚E〛—dc22 2005035449. Manufactured in China. Set in Kennerly. 10 9 8 7 6 5 4 3 2 1

*For everything there is a season, and a time for
every purpose under heaven.*
—Ecclesiastes 3:1, ASV

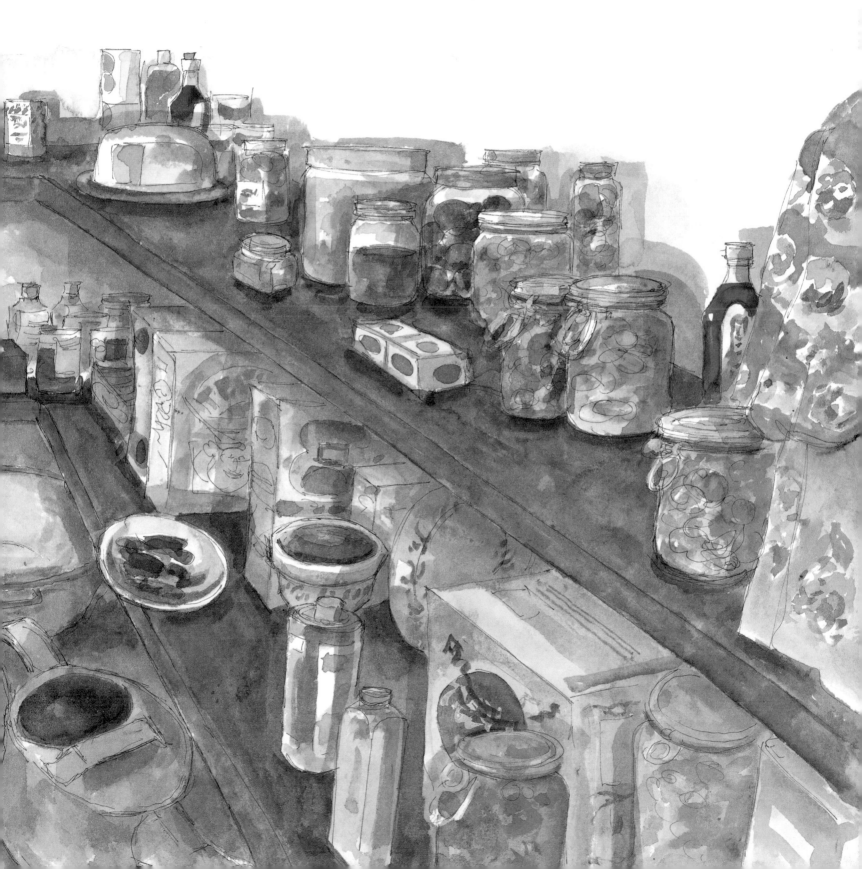

$\mathcal{V}$iolet and her brother and sister were born in the kitchen pantry of a house on top of a hill.

For days, an old crate lined with scraps of calico was the kittens' entire world. But soon, they were strong enough to nose around the pantry, and then the vast kitchen that lay beyond the door.

The kittens were quick to invent games for themselves, like chasing after the broom as Cook swept the floor, or pouncing on the occasional pea or potato that rolled off the counter. Then one day, without warning, Violet's brother, Samson, launched himself at Cook's foot as she walked by.

Violet watched as her brother held fast to Cook's shoe. "What game is that?" she asked her sister, Daisy.

"It's not a game," said Daisy. "He's learning how to catch a mouse."

"Why would he want to catch a mouse?" Violet watched as Cook reached down and plucked Samson from her foot.

"Because mice are the enemy," said Violet's mother. "They steal food from pantries, they chew holes in linens. . . . Why, they've even been known to eat through books! It's our job to kill them."

Violet's eyes widened. *Kill them?*

"Don't worry, Violet," said her mother. "Mousing comes naturally to us. Just remember the rules: 'Prowl silently. Plan your leap carefully. And pounce boldly.' It will happen in time, you'll see."

It wasn't long before the kittens began to look like cats. Daisy's spindly tail became long and lush. Samson's big paws grew bigger still. Violet's downy fur turned as white as fresh milk, and she took care to groom each hair neatly into place.

Violet's mother had been preparing her kittens for the day they would go out and find their places in the world. So they were eager and curious when Cook led a group of strangers to the pantry door.

"It's time, my little ones," said Violet's mother. She gathered the kittens around her, licking each of their heads lovingly. "Come back and visit me, and remember the rules."

"This one here is Daisy," Cook said. Violet watched as a pair of big hands reached for her sister.

"That's the doctor," her mother whispered as Daisy was carried away. "A mouse was spotted in his waiting room."

A woman in a tidy apron plucked Violet's brother from the crate. "Oh yes, Samson's a good one," Cook told the woman. "Just look at those paws."

"She owns the grocery," said Violet's mother. "There are lots of mice in the storeroom."

Finally, there was just one stranger left, and Violet sat up as tall as she could. If this was the person for her, she wanted to look her very best.

"See the dirt under his nails?" whispered Violet's mother. "He runs the nursery."

Violet looked at her mother, puzzled. What was a nursery? Did it have mice? How would she be able to keep her white fur clean in a dirty place?

"Violet's little," said Cook, "but she's a special one."

The man lifted Violet from the crate and peered into her bright green eyes. "I suppose a little mouse catcher is better than none at all," he said.

"Be brave," Violet's mother meowed as the man carried Violet away. "And remember the rules!"

Although the gardener whistled cheerfully all the way down the hill, Violet couldn't keep from trembling. She missed her mother!

When they finally came to a stop and she dared to take a peek, she was amazed. Long tables held trays bright with petunias, geraniums, and pansies, while nearby butterfly bushes gave off a heavenly scent.

The gardener set Violet on top of a counter next to a rack filled with seed packets.

"Guard these well, Violet. Mice love to chew holes in seed packets. Especially the sunflower seeds."

Next he showed Violet her food bowls and a basket where she would sleep.

All day long, a bell jangled above the door as people came and went. Violet leaped from table to table to help the customers select their plants, but no one seemed to want her suggestions.

She tried to help the gardener straighten the wobbly rows of clay pots, but he placed her on the floor. "Not now, Violet," he said. "I've got my job to do, and you've got yours."

That night, as Violet lay in her basket, she heard a *scritch, scritch* from above her.

A small shape moved across the countertop. A mouse!

Violet leaped up and scrambled after the mouse as it raced toward the seed packets. The gardener's sunflower seeds! Violet had to save them.

*Crash!* went the seed rack as Violet dove after the mouse.

*Rat-tat-tat!* went the rakes.

*Smash! Smash! CRASH!* went the wobbly clay pots.

When it was all over, the mouse was long gone, and Violet crept back to her basket, miserable.

She'd forgotten rule number one: Prowl silently.

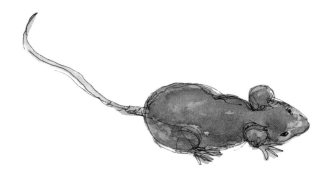

The next morning, the gardener took one look at the mess and frowned. "I'm afraid this won't do," he said, shaking his head. "I need a cat to catch mice, not turn my shop upside down."

And so the gardener carried Violet back to the house on the hill.

Cook frowned at her return, but Violet's mother licked her happily.

"Don't worry," said her mother. "God has a plan for each of us. The right person will come for you."

The very next morning, Cook led a woman in a starched white hat to the pantry.

"It's the baker," said Violet's mother. "Lots of breadcrumbs means lots of mice!"

The baker studied Violet closely. "Well, she's a little one, but I suppose a little mouse catcher is better than none at all." And with that, the baker tucked Violet under her arm and headed out the door.

"Keep your paws clean!" Violet's mother meowed after them. "And remember the rules!"

The bakery reminded Violet of Cook's kitchen. Heat ribboned out from the oven doors, and the air was filled with the scent of fresh bread and spices. The baker showed Violet a stack of empty flour bags where she was to sleep and bowls where her food was kept.

All day long, a bell above the door chimed as people came and went. Violet curled around the customers' legs as they peered into the display cases. She knew the custard tarts were delicious (she'd sampled a bit of custard when the baker wasn't looking), but when she meowed to let the customers know, no one paid her much attention.

When Violet tried to help the baker knead the bread dough, she was shooed off the countertop. "Not now, Violet," the baker said. "I've got my job to do, and you've got yours."

That night, after the ovens had cooled and Violet was asleep on her flour sacks, a familiar *scritch, scritch* awoke her.

Sure enough, a mouse darted from beneath the oven.

Violet crept toward the bread case. *Rule number one: Prowl silently.*

*Rule number two . . . What was it again? Plan something, but plan what?* As her feet touched the countertop, Violet began to slide.

*Bam! Bam!* went a stack of baking sheets.

*Thump! Thump! Thump!* went a dozen loaves of bread.

*Ka-POOF!* went a bag of flour.

The mouse was long gone. Disappointed in herself, Violet settled back on top of her flour sacks. *Plan your leap carefully.* Now she remembered.

The next morning, the baker looked at the flour-covered kitchen. "Oh, no!" she said. "I'm afraid this won't do. I need a cat to catch mice, not turn my bakery upside down."

And so the baker tucked Violet under her arm like a little loaf of white bread and walked back to the house on the hill.

"I remembered rule number one," Violet told her mother. "But I forgot rule number two. Why can't I figure out what God has planned for me?"

"Be patient," said Violet's mother. "It's hard to recognize His plan while we're in the midst of it."

Later that day, a lady came to look into the crate. She had clean hands, unlike the gardener. And instead of a starchy white hat like the baker, she wore her hair loose. Around her neck were strings of colorful beads that shimmered in the sunlight.

"Aren't you a lovely one!" the lady said as she stroked Violet's back. Violet felt a purr begin to rumble in her throat.

"Violet's an extra fine cat, Miss Alice," said Cook.

"In that case, I promise to take extra good care of her."

"I don't know this one," Violet's mother meowed, "but have faith!"

Alice carried Violet down the hill to a building with gold lettering across the window. Inside, the air smelled of paper and beeswax and tea. Brightly colored books lined shelves along the walls. Alice pointed out sections for history, art, cooking, literature, gardening, and poetry. There were even books for children, and of all the books in the shop, Violet thought they were the most beautiful.

Later, Alice showed Violet a fluffy cushion where she was to sleep and a mismatched set of bowls where her food would be kept. Alice smoothed the fur on Violet's head and scratched her gently behind her ears. Just then, a bell rang out. "That would be a customer!" said Alice. "Let's give her a warm welcome, shall we?"

All day long, the bell above the door tinkled as people came and went. Violet followed the customers as they moved through the maze of shelves. She studied the books backward and forward and upside down. And after each customer paid, Violet worked hard to pull the receipt tape from the register.

"Thank you, Violet," Alice always said. "What would I do without such a helpful cat?"

It was a busy, happy day, and yet, Violet couldn't help but worry. She knew Alice would eventually want her to catch mice, just as the gardener and the baker had done.

That night as Violet was settling down to sleep, she saw something move along the floor. *It's just a stray book receipt*, she told herself.

But when the something turned and moved the other way, Violet sat up—it was no receipt! And hadn't Mother said that mice even ate books? The rules! What was she supposed to do?

*Prowl silently.*

Violet crept forward as quietly as a moonbeam through a window.

*Plan your leap carefully.*

Violet tensed herself like an arrow about to be shot from a bow.

What came next? Yes! *Pounce boldly!*

Violet closed her eyes and pounced. When she opened them again, she was amazed to see a tail beneath her paw. And connected to the tail was . . . a mouse.

She had caught a mouse at last!

It was small and gray, with twinkling eyes and a pink nose that quivered with fear. *This* tiny thing was the enemy?

Suddenly the light went on. "Violet!" exclaimed Alice. "What are you doing?"

Violet blinked. She knew Alice expected her to finish off the mouse; after all, it was her job.

Violet felt a terrible sadness because she knew what she had to do. And with that she lifted her paw . . .

. . . and let the mouse go.

"Come here, Violet," said Alice.

Violet took one last look around the bookstore. Of all the places she had been, she liked this one best.

"I'm so glad you let that little mouse go," Alice said.

Violet jumped onto Alice's lap and looked at her curiously. Wasn't Alice going to send her away? Hadn't she failed once again as a mouse catcher?

Alice held her close. "Mice are nuisances. But they're God's creatures, too. We'll find other ways of keeping them out."

The next day, Violet helped Alice find all the holes in the floorboards and baseboards where a mouse might sneak in. Then they plugged the holes with rags.

"What would I do without such a helpful cat?" said Alice. "I'm so glad you've come to stay."

Violet purred with contentment. Her mother was right. God had a plan for her all along, and it suited Violet just fine.